To the Children of Morelia.
And to all those who are moving in search
of a life without fear.

mexique

A REFUGEE STORY FROM THE SPANISH CIVIL WAR

MARÍA JOSÉ FERRADA · ANA PENYAS

TRANSLATED BY
ELISA AMADO

EERDMANS BOOKS FOR YOUNG READERS
GRAND RAPIDS, MICHIGAN

At night I close my eyes and feel the waves beating.

I think they are saying something to the ship.

Mexique. That's what it is called.

Do the waves know that?

Does the sea keep the names of all the ships?

I can't really remember where it is we are going,

but it is far.

We will be there until everything calms down.

Three or four months.

Like an extra-long summer vacation. That's what my mother said.

My mother, who whispered "my child" when she hugged me goodbye.

1, 2, 3…
78, 79, 80…
221, 222, 223…
312, 313, 314…
409, 410, 411…
456 boys and girls on board.

War is a very loud noise.
War is a huge hand that shakes you
and throws you onto a ship.

We set sail, and the grown-ups stay behind on the shore until they are tiny.
Fathers and mothers are stars now that you can see in the distance,
fires that someone lit a million years ago.

A hand takes hold of me.

A hand that ends in the body of a girl.

Because there are the big ones, and there are the small ones.

The small ones attach ourselves to sisters

we didn't have before.

Mine is eleven or twelve.

Her name is Clara.

Sometimes we sing.
One begins, and the rest follow.
Songs bloom like flowers.
The songs have always been in our pockets,
in the few clothes we are bringing.

What is the Republic?

The Republic is a house.

The Republic is a raised fist. A bird.

There are big wars and small ones.

(456 boys and girls on board.)

Because there are the big ones, and there are the small ones.

And the suitcases of the big ones grow.

Those of the small ones shrink

like the moon we can see at night from the ship.

Could it be the same moon that lit up the sky back there?

The same one that you can see from the windows of my house?

Some cry. Especially at night.
They say they dream that the ground is crumbling.
The houses are crumbling, and their memories are blank.
Clara, Sonia, Eulalia, María wake us up.
They say it's just a dream,
one that we all dream together.
Clara, Sonia, Eulalia, María, our sisters,
collect our tears in their handkerchiefs and in the morning
return them to the sea.

The sea is a place
that never ends.

We play at imagining where we are going:

Morelia is a color.

Morelia is the name of a soft animal.

Morelia is a fruit.

We know we are getting closer
because, far away, white handkerchiefs are waving.
From a distance, the handkerchiefs look like the flags of a country without a name.
From a distance, the white handkerchiefs look like stars or flowers.

In the crowd, I hold my suitcase tight
(a suitcase is also a clump of earth, a house).
In the crowd, I lose Clara's hand.
We move forward. We think that the war stayed behind.
But it's not true—we bring the war in our suitcases.

Three or four months. Like summer vacation, only longer.
Do the waves know that?
Will the sea keep the history of all the ships?

AFTERWORD

On May 27, 1937, the ship *Mexique* set sail from Bordeaux, France, on its way to Mexico.

There were 456 children on board, all children of Spanish Republicans. In Mexico they would seek refuge from the Spanish Civil War that battered their country. For more than a year, Spain had been at war with itself. One side, the side of General Francisco Franco, fought for monarchy—for Spain to be ruled by kings and priests. The other side, the side of the Republicans, fought for democracy—for Spain to be ruled by the people.

The war was violent and terrifying. Cities were under attack. Children had to learn how to survive bombings. They would run for shelter and hide in basements or subway stations. Parents worried that their children would be killed, so they made the decision to send them away, out of the war zone. "Three or four months," said mothers and fathers as they hugged their children for the last time. That was the plan. They all thought that the war would end soon, and that they would see each other again.

On June 7, 1937, the children disembarked in Veracruz, Mexico. They were received by cheering crowds waving white handkerchiefs. Many Mexicans, including President

Lázaro Cárdenas, agreed with the Spanish Republicans, and they received these children as if they were war heroes. The voyage then continued by train to Morelia, Michoacán, on the other side of Mexico.

The children disembarked without knowing that History, the one written with a capital letter, would take charge of their plans and turn them into the "Children of Morelia." They did not know that the defeat of the Spanish Republic would turn this short period into a permanent exile. When Francisco Franco's forces won the war, he sought vengeance against anyone who opposed him. He threw his enemies in prison or ordered their execution. Spain could be deadly for Republicans and their families. And Spain had spent all its resources on the war. People no longer had food to eat, jobs to work, or money to spend. Then, five months after the end of the Spanish Civil War, World War II began. Europe had become a dangerous place. The children's parents agreed: the children were better off in Mexico.

It wasn't easy. As months turned into years, the children's worries grew into anxiety and confusion.

The children of Morelia carried pain and trauma from the war with them. The help of the Mexican government—feeding them, finding them a place to live, and educating them—continued until 1948. After that we don't know what happened to each of the children. What we do know is that time passed and most of these children found a way to put down roots in Mexico, build families, and have, as they say, a normal life.

For different reasons, returning to their original home was not easy. The few who tried found themselves in a country with siblings and landscapes that they no longer recognized.

"Where are you from?" Maybe they couldn't even answer that question. Because exile stole that answer from the "Children of Morelia"—and from all children forced to flee their countries and seek refuge elsewhere.

This book is about those who left behind homes that were broken by war, in the hope that fate would give them a life of dignity, the kind of life that all human beings should be able to live.

We tell the story of one ship, knowing that there is no registry of all those who cross the sea, every day, seeking that basic human right: a life without fear.

Eerdmans Books for Young Readers would like to thank Fulbright-National Geographic Digital Storyteller, Destry Maria Sibley, a writer, producer, and descendant of a *Mexique* passenger, for her input and assistance with this project.

A discussion guide with further resources is available through the Eerdmans Books for Young Readers website (eerdmans.com/youngreaders).

First published in the United States in 2020
by Eerdmans Books for Young Readers,
an imprint of Wm. B. Eerdmans Publishing Co.
Grand Rapids, Michigan

www.eerdmans.com/youngreaders

Originally published by
© Alboroto Ediciones, Mexico, 2018
Original title: *Mexique: El nombre del barco*
All rights reserved
Published in agreement with Phileas Fogg Agency
www.phileasfoggagency.com

Manufactured in China.

English-language translation © Elisa Amado 2020

27 26 25 24 23 22 21 20   1 2 3 4 5 6 7 8 9

ISBN 978-0-8028-5545-9

Library of Congress Cataloging-in-Publication Data

Names: Ferrada, María José, 1977- author. | Penyas, Ana, 1987-
    illustrator. | Amado, Elisa, translator.
Title: Mexíque : a refugee story from the Spanish Civil War / María José
    Ferrada, Ana Penyas ; translated by Elisa Amado.
Description: Grand Rapids, Michigan : Eerdmans Books for Young Readers,
    2020. | Audience: Ages 7-10. | Summary: Follows a group of 456 children
    whose families sent them to Mexico aboard the Mexique at the start of
    the Spanish Civil War for what was expected to be a short stay. Includes
    historical notes.
Identifiers: LCCN 2020008121 | ISBN 9780802855459 (hardcover)
Subjects: CYAC: Refugees—Fiction. | Spain—History—Civil War,
    1936-1939—Fiction. | Mexico—History—1910-1946—Fiction.
Classification: LCC PZ7.1.F464 Mex 2020 | DDC [E]—dc23
LC record available at https://lccn.loc.gov/2020008121

María José Ferrada is a Chilean journalist and writer. She is a recipient of the Municipal Prize of Literature of Santiago, as well as the Academy Award from the Chilean Academy of Language. In 2018 she received the Hispanic-American Prize for poetry for children. She currently works as the children's editor of Chilean Memory, a digital resource center of the National Library of Chile.

Ana Penyas has a degree in fine arts from the Polytechnic University of Valencia. In 2018, she was the first woman to win Spain's National Comic Award. She has also received the Josep Toutain Prize for Best New Talent at the International Comic Fair of Barcelona. Raised in Valencia, she now lives in Madrid. Visit Ana's website at anapenyas.es or follow her on Instagram at @ana_penyas.

This book is based on extensive research and interviews, and the images in this book are based on photographs of the "Children of Morelia" and the ship that brought them to Mexico.